Happy Birthday, Baby!

A Bugleberry Book™

Written by Ruth Brook
Illustrated by Vala Kondo

Troll Associates

Library of Congress Cataloging in Publication Data

Brook, Ruth.
  Happy birthday, Baby.

  Summary: The Bugleberries surprise birthday party for
Baby is more a surprise for them than for him.
  [1. Babies—Fiction. 2. Birthdays—Fiction.
3. Parties—Fiction] I. Kondo, Vala, ill. II. Title.
PZ7.B78964Hap   1988   [E]   86-30750
ISBN 0-8167-0912-2 (lib. bdg.)
ISBN 0-8167-0913-0 (pbk.)

One sunny morning, the Bugleberries were marching around Bo's backyard, pretending to be in a parade.

Baby had a cold and could not come out to play.

"Let's bring our parade to Baby," said Bo. "It will cheer him up!"

So they all marched over to Baby's house.

3

Brrump! Brrump! Brrump! Bump! Bump!
Up the stairs and into the nursery the
Bugleberries marched! First came Jingle,
kicking her heels and carrying a bright red
flag. Next came Betty, twirling a baton.
Toony played her little silver triangle, and
Bo blew into his great big tuba. Dolly clicked
her castanets, and Rosie played the flute.

Finally, Skip came marching in, banging
on an old tin drum with long wooden
drumsticks.

Brrump! Brrump! Brrump! Bump! Bump!
Baby clapped his hands and squealed with
delight.

4

The Bugleberries marched around and around, until they were too tired to go on. Then they all flopped down on the floor to rest. They looked around the room.

Baby's room was so different from theirs! There was a crib, and a playpen, and a squeaky toy that looked like a mouse. There were cloth picture books, and big plastic blocks, and even a little rubber ducky!

"Look at all these silly baby toys!" cried Betty.

"*Baby* doesn't think they're silly. He likes them," whispered Toony. But nobody heard her.

6

Then, Rosie noticed a calendar on the wall. A big red circle was drawn around one of the dates. It was marked, *Baby's First Birthday*.

"Look, everybody!" Rosie shouted. "Next Sunday is Baby's birthday! What are we going to do?"

8

"I have an idea," said Dolly. Everyone gathered around her. "Let's have a surprise party for Baby," she whispered.

"Oh, goody!" shouted Toony.

"Goody! Goody!" Baby squealed.

"*Shhh*, Toony!" Jingle said. "We mustn't let Baby hear us. Remember, a surprise party is a secret!"

The next day, the Bugleberries made plans for the party.

"Let's have spaghetti at the party," said Skip. "I love spaghetti!"

"Isn't Baby too little to eat spaghetti?" Toony asked. But Dolly interrupted before anyone could answer.

"I'll bring a pot and some wooden spoons from home," she said. "Then we can cook the spaghetti at Baby's house."

"I'll bring paper placemats," Betty added.

"And we can all go shopping for food and presents this afternoon," said Jingle.

Everyone agreed.

11

12

After lunch, the Bugleberries went to the Accordion Department Store to shop.

Betty saw a pretty pink hat on the counter.

"Oh, how beautiful!" she said. "I think I'll buy it for Baby."

"That hat won't fit Baby," whispered Toony. But everyone was so busy admiring the hat that nobody heard her.

The saleswoman packed Betty's present in a big yellow box. She tied it with a bright purple cord.

In the next department, Bo bought Baby a fishing pole, and Skip bought a big book about sailing.

Toony just looked on. "Baby is too little to go fishing," she muttered, "and he doesn't know how to read. Whatever will Baby do with these presents?"

Rosie bought a bouquet of her favorite flowers. Dolly bought a jar of face cream, and Jingle got a pair of green-and-white woolly socks.

15

At last, they arrived at the Sacks of Fun Supermarket. They loaded their shopping carts with spaghetti, tomato sauce, party favors, and a big birthday cake!

Toony saw a little pink and blue rattle. She bought it for Baby.

On the morning of the party, the Bugleberries brought all the packages to Baby's house. They stuffed them into the hall closet so that Baby wouldn't see. Then they went home to get the birthday cake and change into their party clothes.

18

As soon as the Bugleberries left the house, Baby ran to the closet door. He stood up on his tiptoes and tugged at the door with all his might.

He tugged and tugged.
Suddenly, the door opened, and
all the packages came tumbling out!
"Whee!" said Baby, clapping
his hands.

Baby spread a paper placemat out on the floor. Then he opened the jar of tomato sauce.

"Paint!" said Baby.

He dipped his little fingers into the jar and scooped up a handful of red sauce. Then he painted wide red stripes on the placemat.

"Flag," said Baby.

Next, he opened the jar of face cream and spread it across the fishing pole. He put the placemat on top. The face cream made it stick to the pole. Baby waved his little flag back and forth.

"Whee!" he said.

FACEC

SPAGHETTI

23

Next, Baby opened the big yellow box. He took out the tissue paper and the pretty pink hat.

Then he turned the shiny yellow box upside down and put it on his head.

"Hat," gurgled Baby.

Baby pulled the long woolly socks up over his legs.

"Boots!" he said with glee, as he stomped around the room.

Then Baby saw Dolly's wooden spoons and great big pot. The pot was upside down.

He took the spoons, plopped down next to the pot, and began banging with all his might.

"Drum!" said Baby. "Drum!"

Brrump! Brrump! Brrump! Bump! Bump!

Soon, the Bugleberries arrived at Baby's front door. They were all dressed up in their party clothes, ready to have a great time!

But Toony was sad. "This party is supposed to be a happy surprise for Baby," she cried. "But Baby won't have fun! Babies don't eat spaghetti, or wear big hats, or go fishing, or read books. Babies don't wear long socks, or use face cream!"

Everybody listened and thought about what Toony said.

"I guess it won't be a *happy* birthday for Baby after all!" said Bo.

"Some surprise!" Jingle groaned.

The Bugleberries walked into the house.

"Look!" shouted Jingle. She could hardly believe her eyes.

There, prancing happily around the room, was Baby. He was beating his drum and waving his flag and having a wonderful time!

"Surprise! Surprise!" shouted Baby.

"This *is* a surprise party after all!" said Rosie. "A surprise for *us*!"

Baby climbed up on top of Skip's big book and sat proudly at the head of the table.

Betty brought the birthday cake. The Bugleberries helped Baby blow out the candle. Then they hugged and kissed him and sang, *Happy birthday to you!*

Happy birthday, Baby!

32